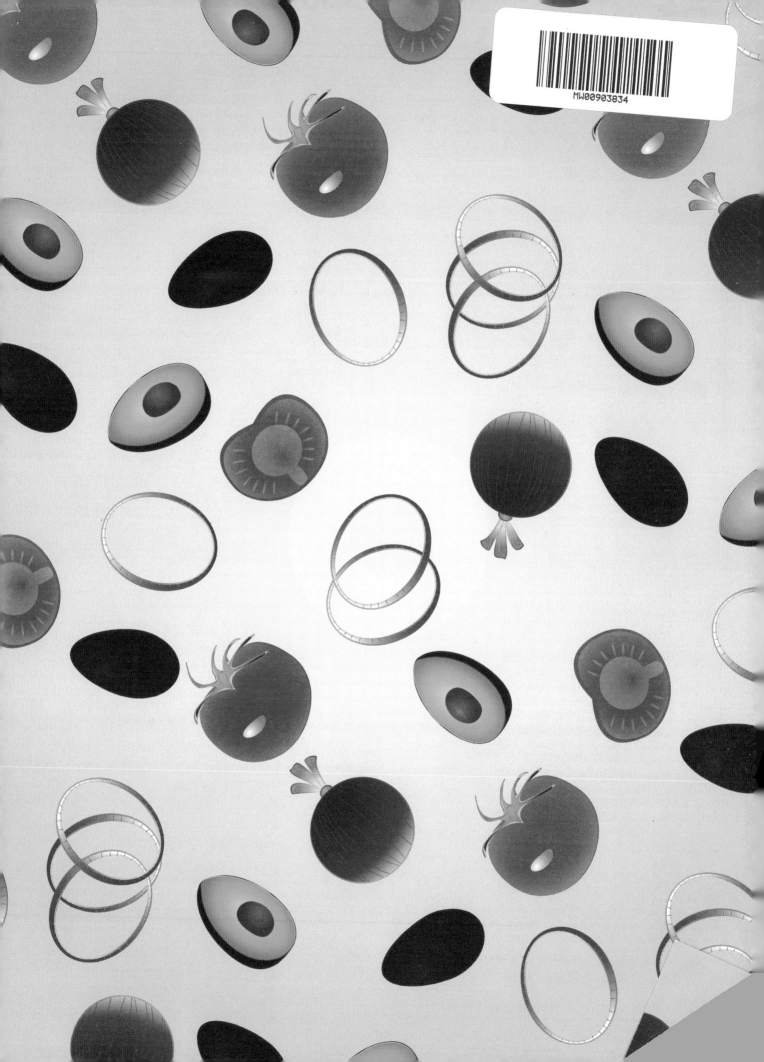

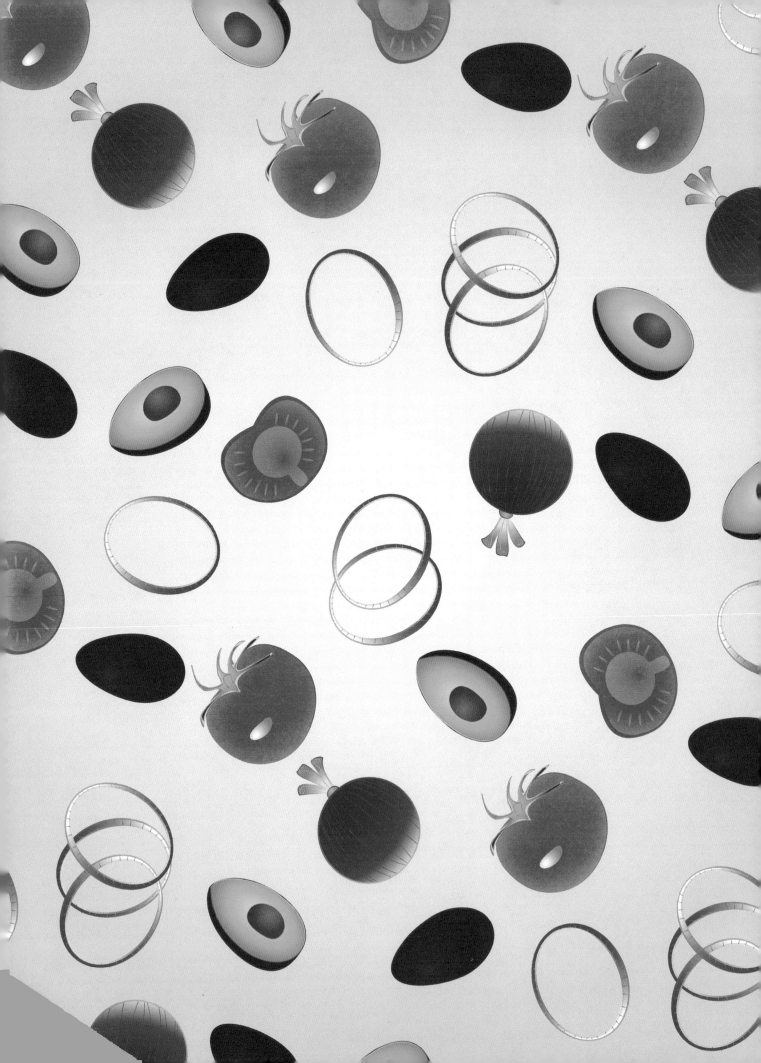

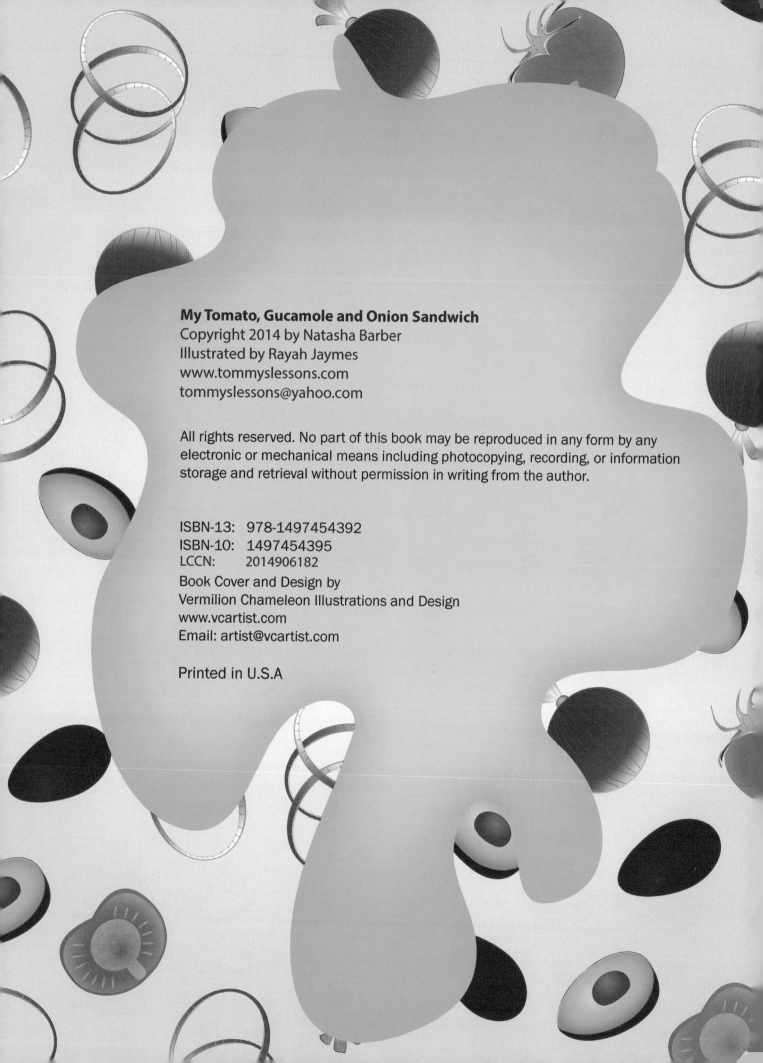

ISBN-13:   978-1497454392
ISBN-10:   1497454395
LCCN: 2014906182
Book Cover and Design by
Vermilion Chameleon Illustrations and Design
www.vcartist.com
Email: artist@vcartist.com

Printed in U.S.A

For Isaac S., Joshua S., Grayson B., and Zach B.

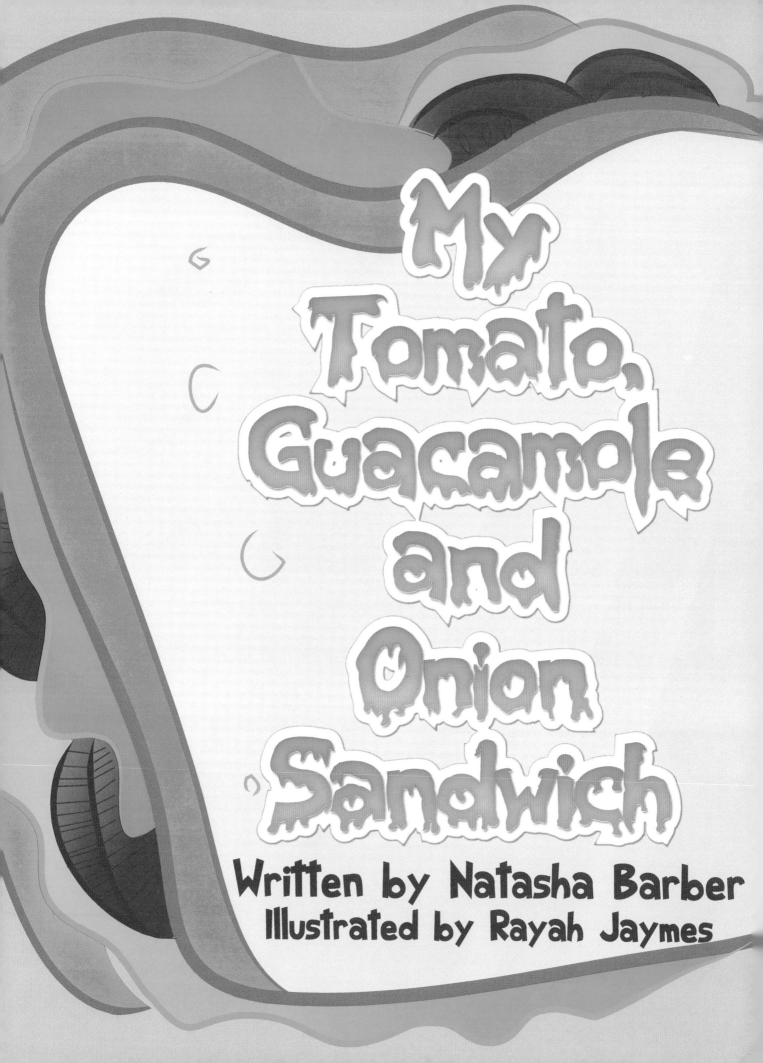

My Tomato, Guacamole and Onion Sandwich

Written by Natasha Barber

Illustrated by Rayah Jaymes

Hello!
My name is Tommy and I am seven years old.
I was wondering something. Have you ever had a
tomato, guacamole, and onion sandwich before?

Well, I hadn't either until I found
one in my lunch one day.
You are probably wondering what I did with
the tomato, guacamole, and onion sandwich.

Well, I quickly stuffed it back
into my lunch box so that no one would see it.
When the bell rang, I ran back to my locker and hid
that tomato, guacamole, and onion sandwich in it.

That afternoon when my mom picked me up from school, she asked me how my day was. I said, "It was a bad day. You packed me the wrong lunch. I got your sandwich by mistake."

My mom said, "What do you mean, hun? You didn't like your sandwich today?" I couldn't **believe** my mom actually thought I would eat a tomato, guacamole, and onion sandwich.

I went to school the next day, and my mom did not send a tomato, guacamole, and onion sandwich with me; but I forgot about the tomato, guacamole, and onion sandwich I put in my locker.

A few days went by. I noticed some fruit flies in my locker and a weird smell; but I did not remember that I had a very old tomato, guacamole, and onion sandwich still hidden in my locker.

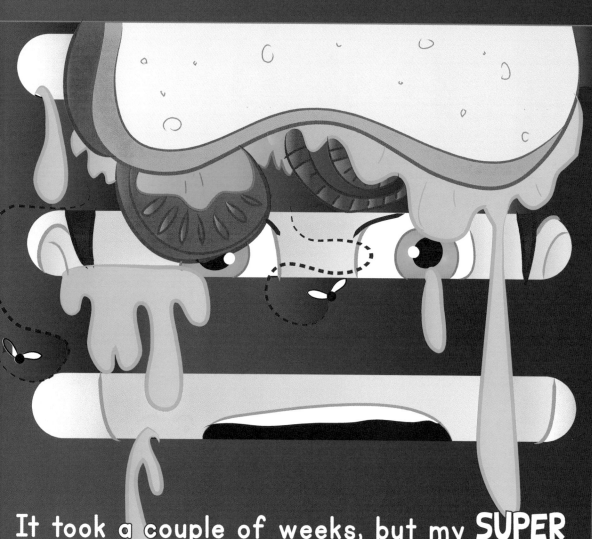

It took a couple of weeks, but my **SUPER** old, **SUPER** stinky tomato, guacamole, and onion sandwich began to slowly **grow** and **grow** and **GROW** until it began to **ooze** out of my locker.

Have you ever seen a
tomato, guacamole, and onion sandwich grow?
Well, I hadn't either until the day I opened my
locker and a **SUPER** mean, **SUPER** ugly
tomato, guacamole, and onion sandwich popped out.

There I stood, *surprised* and terrified of the
tomato, guacamole, and onion sandwich. My
small sandwich was now **SUPER** large, with
eyes and teeth; and it looked **ANGRY**.

I bumped into the principal, Mrs. Backstaple, who was patrolling the hallways. She grabbed a fire extinguisher and we headed for my locker.

The tomato, guacamole, and onion sandwich was now as tall as me, but Mrs. Backstaple didn't care. She released the fire extinguisher on my super ugly, super stinky tomato, guacamole, and onion sandwich.

The tomato, guacamole, and onion sandwich began to fight back. It started to throw pieces of tomato and onion at us. I hid behind Mrs. Backstaple as she continued to spray the sandwich with the fire extinguisher.

By the time she emptied the fire extinguisher, all that was left was soggy bread, watery guacamole, and floating pieces of tomatoes and onions.

Mrs. Backstaple turned to me with a stern face and said, "Tommy, what do you have to say for yourself?"
I said, "Mrs. Backstaple, that was the **meanest** sandwich I have ever met."

As I was sitting in the office in detention, I thought about the very valuable lesson I had learned at school that day.

I am sure you will agree with me on this:

NEVER EVER MIX
tomato,
guacamole
and onion
in a sandwich
again!

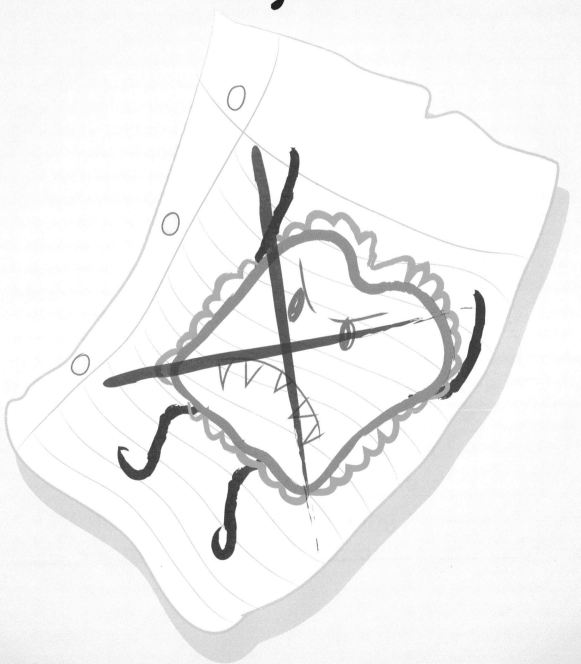

About the Author

Natasha Barber is an Engineer and works in the automotive industry in Michigan.
She is a mother of 4 boys: Isaac S, Joshua S, Grayson B, and Zach B.
Her passion is her family and her kids.
She enjoys being creative and focuses her stories on being whimsical, fun and magical.

About the Illustrator

Rayah Jaymes is an illustrator, chef and musician that comes from an incredibly large multicultral family which continues to inspire her art and story telling. She aspires to illustrate many more books that educate children and their parents about the diverse world around them and how they can make it better everyday in everything they do.
Find her and more of her books at www.vcartist.com

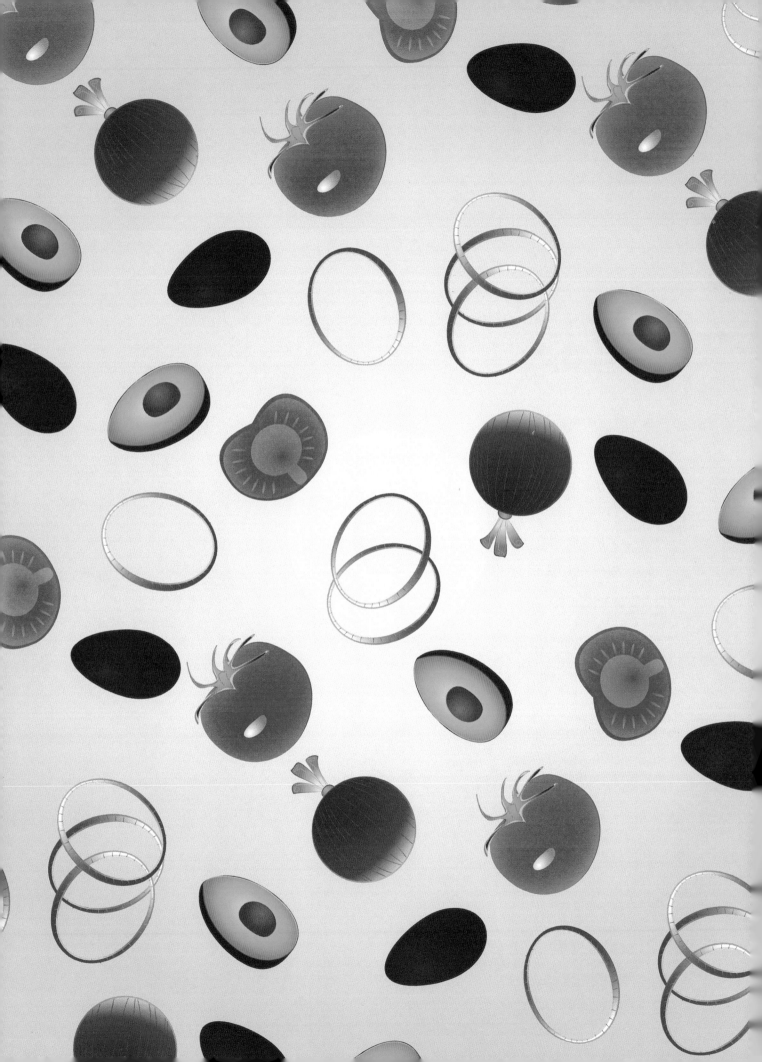

Made in the USA
Lexington, KY
04 May 2014